MW00585522

Orange

by Aditi Brennan Kapil

SAMUELFRENCH.COM   SAMUELFRENCH.CO.UK

FOR PRODUCTION ENQUIRIES

UNITED STATES AND CANADA
Info@SamuelFrench.com
1-866-598-8449

UNITED KINGDOM AND EUROPE
Plays@SamuelFrench.co.uk
020-7255-4302

Each title is subject to availability from Samuel French, depending
upon country of performance. Please be aware that *ORANGE* may
not be licensed by Samuel French in your territory. Professional and
amateur producers should contact the nearest Samuel French office or
licensing partner to verify availability.

MUSIC USE NOTE

IMPORTANT BILLING AND CREDIT REQUIREMENTS

ORANGE premiered at the Mixed Blood Theatre in Minneapolis, Minnesota on November 11, 2016. The performance was directed by Jack Reuler, with set design by Joseph Stanley, costume design by Janet O'Neill, lighting design by Wu Chen Khoo, and sound design by Victor Zupanc. The stage manager was Robin MacGregor. The cast was as follows:

LEELA	Annelyse Ahmad
ALL THE WOMEN	Lipica Shah
ALL THE MEN	Owais Ahmed

ORANGE was commissioned and first produced by South Coast Repertory with support from the Time Warner Foundation. The production premiered on March 5, 2017. The performance was directed by Jessica Kubzansky, with scenic design by Michael B. Raiford, costume design by Denitsa Bliznakova, lighting design by Jaymi Lee Smith, and sound design by John Nobori. The stage manager was Kathryn Davies. The cast was as follows:

LEELA	Pia Shah
ALL THE WOMEN	Anjali Bhimani
ALL THE MEN	Karthik Srinivasan

CHARACTERS

LEELA – Seventeen, South Asian. On autism spectrum.

Everyone else:
Actress – Age range: nine–forty. All the women.
Actor – Age range: eighteen–forty. All the men.

AUTHOR'S NOTES

Some notes on Leela's mythic encounters:

Scene Two, the taxi driver: Casual wisdom from an unexpected source. The more he can throw it away and not play its significance, the better.

Scene Eight, the nine-year-old girl: The showdown of the deadpan and mule-headed at the O.K. Corral, avoid over-decorating the girl, the funny is in how immovably stubborn they both are, not in playing her age or any other facet of her personality.

Scene Nine, the old dude: Deep and cryptic, like the old cowboy you encounter by the fire after three days of walking who probably knows the answer to everything but won't tell you until you prove yourself; slow-talking, evaluating you to see if you're worthy, probably chews tobacco, probably has some stuck on his tongue that he can't quite pick out. But also, he's just the crazy dude who sleeps in the park that you're not supposed to talk to.

Scene Twelve, man and woman: White trash, biker gang demons, all-around bad news. If they were less drunk this might have gotten a lot worse.

General Style Note:

This story is told from the point of view of the central character, Leela, who has a particular lens on the world. Please ensure that even when she is not doing the majority of the talking, her point of view is foregrounded. Upstaging of other actors for dramaturgical purposes is allowed and even recommended.

The characters played by the ensemble, while fully developed and three-dimensional, exist in this play only by way of Leela's relationship with them. Please avoid adding internal information or subtext that does not coincide with Leela's experience of her interaction with them.

Illustrations Note:

Leela's illustrations in the journal that she carries with her throughout provide the scenic backdrop for the play, but Leela interacts with them as though they exist downstage, i.e. somewhere above the audience. They are minimalist at the beginning and gradually evolve in detail, lushness, and beauty over the course of her adventure. In the final scene, they are revealed as simple geometric shapes. For this trick to work, it's best to conceal what she's actually drawing throughout the play.

Illustration cues are in bold and bracketed.

Licensees are not required to use the illustrations included with the play and may create their own.

Scene One: In Air

(In an airplane over the Pacific Ocean. Airplane seats, airplane sound. **MOTHER** *and* **LEELA** *sitting side by side.* **LEELA** *holds a journal and a pen. She draws an airplane window.)*

[Illustration: Double oval airplane window, no shading, no color.]

*(**LEELA** stares downstage, out the porthole window we see illustrated on the backdrop. The following exchange has the distracted silent spaces between two people who have been quiet for hours. It does not seem like an important conversation.)*

LEELA. Flight recorder beacons send a signal for thirty days before batteries die.

MOTHER. What darling?

LEELA. So if a plane crashes you have thirty days to find it, then it stops signaling.

MOTHER. Okay.

LEELA. But after thirty days you don't expect to find living people in the ocean. But they want to find the black box which tells you the answers to why it happened. That's the important part.

MOTHER. Mm.

LEELA. The black box is actually orange.

MOTHER. What?

LEELA. The black box is orange.

MOTHER. Is that true?

LEELA. Yes.

MOTHER. Okay. Well. That makes sense.

    (Beat.)

So what are you looking at out there?

LEELA. The Pacific Ocean.

MOTHER. Can you see it?

LEELA. No. It's just clouds.

MOTHER. Okay, and if you look up?

LEELA. More clouds.

MOTHER. Keep looking.

LEELA. Why?

MOTHER. It's not often you're above the clouds. Maybe you'll get lucky.

LEELA. How?

MOTHER. Maybe you'll see something you've never seen before.

LEELA. Like what?

MOTHER. The gods must live somewhere. No one has found Mount Meru on earth, so perhaps up here?

LEELA. Really?

MOTHER. I don't know. But if you spot any, give them a message for me, we could use some assistance.

LEELA. Assistance.

MOTHER. Never mind. I miss your grandfather, that's all. You don't have to worry, everything will be fine.
What an adventure, right? We are having an adventure, you and I.

    (Silence.)

Are you watching?

LEELA. Yes.

MOTHER. Okay.

    (Airplane noise rises. Scene transforms to...)

Scene Two: John Wayne Airport

(Loud sounds of cars and honking.)

*(**MOTHER** and **LEELA** are outside airport with luggage. It's misty and cold. **MOTHER** looks around impatiently, **LEELA** gazes at the fog, considers drawing.)*

[No illustration.]

MOTHER. If your father does not come soon, we will take a taxi...

Leela. Leela, don't draw right now, we need to concentrate, okay?

LEELA. Okay.

MOTHER. It's so chilly, California should be warm. It's a good thing we had woollens in the carry-on...

Where is he...

–

What an adventure, huh Leela? Such an adventure.

LEELA. It's not an adventure, it's a street.

MOTHER. What?

LEELA. An adventure is when you go exploring and things happen.

MOTHER. Well this is as adventurous as we are going to get. I don't want you wandering off while we are here, okay? This is a foreign country, and you don't always recognize bad people. I need you to concentrate and keep out of trouble.

LEELA. Okay.

MOTHER. We must summon our resources, yes? Both of us. Summon our resources, find our strength.

LEELA. Call upon the gods for assistance, like in the stories.

MOTHER. Exactly like in Grandfather's stories, in the end the gods come, the battle is won, and everyone is saved.

LEELA. In Grandfather's stories the adventures have jungles and danger.

MOTHER. That is not the sort of adventure we will have, I am serious about this Leela, okay?

LEELA. Okay...

MOTHER. Okay?

(Annoyed now.) Okay, where is he...

(For **LEELA***'s benefit.)* We have made it to California, now we will locate your father, we will conquer all obstacles along the way, the gods will smile on us, and we will be successful.

LEELA. How?

MOTHER. To start with...we will take a taxi.

(She spots a free taxi.)

Okay, hello!

TAXI DRIVER. *(Offstage.)* Taxi?

MOTHER. Yes, are you free?

TAXI DRIVER. *(Offstage.)* Yeah, let's go!

LEELA. The clouds are close.

MOTHER. What?

LEELA. The clouds are close to the ground.

*(***TAXI DRIVER*** enters, grabs a bag.)*

MOTHER. Yes it's very chilly, I had forgotten about the fog.

TAXI DRIVER. That's not fog, that's the marine layer

MOTHER. What?

TAXI DRIVER. The marine layer. It'll burn off by mid-morning. It's temperature inversion, what happens is the cool water meets the warm air, and the air gets thicker than the warmer air above it and gets trapped between land and sky. When the sun gets hot enough it'll burn off.

*(***MOTHER*** and **LEELA** stare at him.)*

Over here.

*(***TAXI DRIVER*** exits.)*

LEELA. Do you think that's how the gods travel? On the clouds, like an elevator? I can send them a message, I have paper...

MOTHER. Okay, maybe later, we need to go.

LEELA. ...Summon them

MOTHER. Your father will like this. This will be a nice surprise.

(**MOTHER** *exits.* **LEELA** *remains, looking up, watchful.*)

(Offstage.) Leela!

(Scene transforms to...)

Scene Three: The Hotel Room

(*A hotel room.* **MOTHER** *and* **FATHER** *argue in the background while* **LEELA**, *foregrounded, draws a window throughout the scene and looks out it.*)

meansid escape

[Illustration: A square with several lines gradually makes a window. There's some basic shading, but no color.]

(**LEELA** *pointedly ignores the fight, which proceeds with no regard for her presence.*)

FATHER. You can't just send one e-mail, and then get on a plane!

LEELA. (*To herself.*) No oranges.

MOTHER. But I can and I have. You may witness the evidence.

LEELA. (*To herself.*) I thought there would be oranges.

FATHER. (*To* **LEELA.**) You want oranges? We'll buy you some. (*To* **MOTHER.**) Nothing here is prepared for you, we are not prepared for you, or for her.

LEELA. On trees.

FATHER. What?

LEELA. Oranges on trees

FATHER. (*To* **LEELA.**) We can buy some, okay? How was your flight? It was good? Did you like the airport? John Wayne Airport? Did you say hello to John Wayne?

LEELA. No. He wasn't there.

FATHER. Okay, well maybe he went for a walk.

MOTHER. She's seventeen, not five.

FATHER. She liked it. She thought it was funny. Right, Leela?

LEELA. Yes.

FATHER. (*To* **MOTHER.**) This is not some vacation, there are many people at this wedding, a number of my business associates, it is not just some family event.

MOTHER. I grew tired of waiting for you.

FATHER. I have been busy, okay?

MOTHER. And why are we staying at this hotel?

FATHER. It's lucky they could even find you a room, you weren't expected.

MOTHER. Why are we not staying at your flat with you?

FATHER. You're not listening! I am working, I am working this whole weekend, this is not the time!

MOTHER. *(Ignoring him.)* Well, I can unpack things later, there is plenty of time.

FATHER. Listen, the plan was that I come to Calcutta and we discuss things properly before any rash action.

MOTHER. Rash action? It has been three months! I have been waiting for you to come to us for three months! In an empty house with my father's things all around to remind me that the only other adult help I had is gone, a daughter with her head in the clouds, and a husband who hardly answers his telephone! I am finished waiting! You are a husband and a father.

FATHER. And you are emotional and reacting irrationally to difficult circumstances, but this is not the answer, uprooting Leela is not the answer, we agreed to a plan!

MOTHER. You agreed, I agreed to nothing.

FATHER. So you arrive in the middle of a wedding?

MOTHER. My niece's wedding! Which I am attending, you can do as you please. But I will not sit quietly any longer. Now I am going to pay my respects to our hosts.

FATHER. What about Leela?

MOTHER. What about her?

FATHER. She can't stay here.

MOTHER. Leela, do you want to pay your respects?

FATHER. You cannot leave!

MOTHER. Leela.

> (**LEELA** *stops drawing, the window is unfinished.*)

LEELA. Yes?

MOTHER. Do you want to pay your respects?

LEELA. No.

MOTHER. Okay.

FATHER. Stop, she is your responsibility, you chose to drag her here!

MOTHER.	**FATHER.**
(To **FATHER**.) I will thank them for the hotel room.	You will not leave

FATHER. Wait!

> (**MOTHER** *exits, door click,* **LEELA** *resumes drawing.*)

Dammit.

> (**FATHER** *is left alone with* **LEELA**. *He doesn't know what to do. Finally...*)

(To **LEELA**.) Can you be alone?

> (*No response.*)

Leela! Can you be alone?

LEELA. No.

FATHER. Dammit.

> (*He's trapped.*)

Okay...what an adventure you're having, huh? What are you...doing over there?

LEELA. There are no oranges here.

FATHER. Do you want me to check with room service? They must have some.

LEELA. (*Interested.*) Really?

FATHER. Yeah sure...

> (*He finds a phone, calls.*)

Hello, room service? Do you have oranges?
Oranges.
No, not oranJUICE, orangES, the fruit, not the liquid.
I don't know, however you have them.

Yes. Yes. OKAY.

(He hangs up, looks at **LEELA**.*)*

Okay.

Good?

LEELA. There are many oranges in Orange County, but no real ones. Not yet.

FATHER. Oh yeah? Listen, I have business, so you will have to stay here in the room for a bit...

LEELA. Orange Bible Church. Orange Realty. Orange You Glad Café. Orange Glaze Nails.

FATHER. Mm. There is also a town.

LEELA. Really?

FATHER. And you were born at the Orange County Medical Center.

LEELA. Mother told me.

FATHER. That was a day. That was a big day. The day you were born. That was...

LEELA. 3:47 a.m.

FATHER. Yes?

LEELA. That's night. Not day.

FATHER. It was an expression. Not a... *[handwritten: She's def on-the spectrum]*

(Knock.)

Okay...here we go

*(***FATHER** *exits, a brief exchange at the door, he re-enters with an orange, hands it to* **LEELA**.*)*

LEELA. A real orange. Thank you.

FATHER. Are you going to eat it?

LEELA. Maybe later

FATHER. Okay. Later.

That's a nice smile you have. Very pretty.

(He tries to control the situation.)

Okay Leela, there are a lot of people here this weekend, and your mother has brought you here... I don't know how you'll...

It's best if you say little, okay? That is for all the young people, best they say little, that is most charming in a young person. Okay?

LEELA. Okay.

(Okay, the situation seems controlled.)

FATHER. You've grown so much. You're very beautiful.

(LEELA pays no attention to him, leaving private space for a memory to encroach.)

You always were lovely...very quiet. When you were two years old I remember we had all the cousins over to play, and you were so serious. None of the aunties could make you laugh. Just looking all the time, very serious, none of the sweet chatter like other children. I remember one lady said, "This child does not like me at all!" And everyone laughed, and your mother and I laughed too but we wondered, you were our first, we did not know you were so different, how should we now...

(He snaps out of it.)

It's okay, you are a unique person.

There are many people here this weekend, Daddy has business associates, okay?

So we will say how shy you are and it will all be fine. It will all be fine.

But Daddy will be very busy, okay? I won't have much time to be with you. You won't mind.

LEELA. No.

FATHER. You eat that, it's good for the bones.

(FATHER starts to leave.)

LEELA. The eyes.

FATHER. What?

LEELA. And the skin. And blood vessels, tendons, and ligaments. And scurvy. It doesn't do much for bones. Calcium is good for bones. Maybe you meant calcium because they both start with C.

FATHER. Okay.
Okay.

> (FATHER *exits. The door clicks.* LEELA *is alone.
> She notices.*)

LEELA. Calcium is good for other things too. Like teeth.
And nerves and muscles.

> *(Pause.)*

Nerves and muscles are good for things. Like running.
And climbing. And sensing danger.

> (LEELA *looks at the orange.* LEELA *draws the
> orange.*)

**[Illustration: A circle, some shading, a little bit
of orange coloring seeps into the circle.]**

> (LEELA *smiles.*)

A real orange.

> *(Scene transforms to...)*

Scene Four: The Dance Club

(Music, lights, dance club, all the wedding guests are having loud, raucous, dancing fun.* **LEELA** *watches.)*

[No illustration.]

*(**PRITI** and **LEELA** have to yell over the music to be heard.)*

PRITI. *(Offstage.)* Hey! You Leela? Hey!

*(**LEELA** looks at **PRITI**.)*

Hey, you Leela? I'm Priti! We're cousins, like second or third I think.

LEELA. Hi.

PRITI. So this place is full of old people, right?

LEELA. Yes.

PRITI. Old people dancing, it's like the third circle of hell or something.

You want to get out of here?

LEELA. What?

PRITI. You know. Escape hell. We can make a break for it.

*(**PRITI** spots her dad on the dance floor.)*

Oh hell no, my dad's gonna breakdance...every damn party...

LEELA. Your dad?

PRITI. Over there. Every party, he gets everyone to form a circle around him and he's all b-boying it down to the ground except these days he can't get back up, so he's down there forever and then after a while it gets obvious that he's not coming back up and everyone sort

---

*A license to produce *Orange* does not include a performance license for any third-party or copyrighted music. Licensees should create an original composition or use music in the public domain. For further information, please see Music Use Note on page 3.

of acts like they're distracted while he gets up off the damn ground so he won't be embarrassed.

What about me? I'm embarrassed!

(**LEELA** *stares out at the dance floor.*)

It's 'cause he's fat.

(**LEELA** *re-focuses on* **PRITI.**)

LEELA. What?

PRITI. I said my dad's fat. But like in his head he's still studly and it's still the eighties. I mean we have mirrors in the house, look in one.

LEELA. Okay.

PRITI. So, you wanna?

LEELA. Wanna what?

PRITI. Get out of here?

LEELA. Why?

PRITI. Why? Why not? 'Cause it'll be fun, that's why.

(*Beat.*)

LEELA. On an adventure?

PRITI. What? An...

–

Sure. Yeah, an adventure. See, I have the pass code out of hell.

LEELA. Pass code?

PRITI. Yeah, my sister, the bride, wants me to do this thing for her, and no one's gonna argue with the bride, not even my mom, so we're totally clear to go. I rue the day I got my license and my sister figured out she could send me on errands, but in this one instance, it's working in our favor. See I've got plans.

LEELA. Plans?

PRITI. A list of places and things I need to check off before I kiss Orange County goodbye for good. It's a ceremonial thing, I leave right after the wedding, so tonight's the night. Anyway, point is you should come, we'll hang out.

And we can take our time too, we'll grab my boyfriend, make our own scene. That looks like something other than this hell dimension.

LEELA. Your boyfriend?

PRITI. On and off. He's cool though, you'll like him. So you coming or no? I can promise it'll be a hell of a lot more fun than this mess.

Or you can stay here and be all good little Indian girl wallpaper if you'd prefer, I mean it's nice, you're decorative.

    (Beat.)

LEELA. Okay.

PRITI. Okay? Okay! Cool! Let's git.

    (Party sounds rise. Scene transforms to...)

Scene Five: The Blimp Hangars

(**PRITI** *stands on the front hood of a convertible, sucking on a Nutella packet.* **LEELA** *sits in the front seat. Or if there's no hood,* **PRITI** *stands on the front seat and* **LEELA** *is in the back. Regardless,* **LEELA** *is somehow separate.*)

(**LEELA** *draws a series of diamonds.*)

[Illustration: A series of diamonds make up a chain-link fence. This illustration expands to include the blimp hangars in Tustin behind the chain-link fence. It is more elaborate than previous drawings, more shading, more color.]

(**PRITI** *honks the car horn to get* **GAR**'s *attention.*)

PRITI. Hey!

GAR. *(Offstage.)* This grass is wet!

(**GAR** *enters, tromps over to the car. He's in sweats, also sucking on a Nutella packet, his shoes are soaked.*)

PRITI. Anything?

GAR. No, I told you, it's like no trespassing all around

PRITI. *(Hollers.)* It's 'cause they don't want us to find the aliens!

GAR. *I* don't want to find the aliens.
    (Re: Nutella.) This Nutella is rank.

PRITI. That's 'cause it's vintage

GAR. I can't believe you kept these.

PRITI. See now, I can't believe you didn't keep yours. We could just break in, I mean what's the worst that can happen?

LEELA. You can be captured and killed.

PRITI. By...who? What?

LEELA. I think that's the worst. Maybe there is something worse.

PRITI. *(To* LEELA.*)* Yeah? You should try to think of something worse. For real, like in great detail!

(GAR *does martial arts moves.*)

GAR. Whachaaah! Whachaaah!

PRITI. *(To* LEELA.*)* That was funny, what I said, did you get that? Do you get funny?

LEELA. No.

PRITI. *(To* GAR.*)* What are you doing?

GAR. You know it's too bad we don't have binoculars, we could observe the alien activity from a safe fenced out distance.

PRITI. You get that a chickenshit attitude completely defeats the purpose of going on an adventure, right?

LEELA. Yes.

GAR. A chickenshit attitude is what saves us from our intestines exploding when the eggs hatch and tentacles crawl out of our eyeballs.

LEELA. What aliens?

PRITI. That's just...what? That's just anatomically unsound, why would tentacles come out of our eyeballs?

GAR. They're aliens.

LEELA. Where?

GAR. Look at those things, there's obviously something messed up going on inside. Whachaaah!

LEELA. Whachah.

GAR. The sound of vanquishing. Whaa!

PRITI. You know what my mom says they are?

GAR. No, no, nah, nah, nah, nah!

PRITI. But for real, she said they're / –

GAR. Nope!

LEELA. *(To* GAR.*)* Are you going to fight the aliens?

PRITI. So for real, you don't want to know what they are, you just want to live in ignorance?

GAR. It's not ignorance, it's believing my eyes and not some government conspiracy.

PRITI. You're such a child

GAR. I mean look at them, weird ass bulbous protrusions... I mean look at the size of them, you could store a fleet of spaceships in there.

PRITI. Fine, so let's go see!

LEELA. Okay.

GAR. No.

PRITI. Why not??

GAR. I am not breaking in, you're going to have to come to terms with this is as close as we get!

PRITI. You're such a quitter.

GAR. Check it off the list, let's move on.

PRITI. I don't think this warrants checking anything off anything, the whole point was we confirm or deny, that's what we wrote.

GAR. Check it off the list.

LEELA. What is the list?

GAR. It's just a list, we made it when we were twelve.

PRITI. Stop talking to her.

GAR. Why?

PRITI. She doesn't need to know, that's all.

GAR. Then why'd you bring her?

PRITI. Can we get back to these two oversized cement toilet rolls and how we need to investigate / –

GAR. No, it's not like I wanted to come out tonight, and if it's going to be all weird and awkward because you've got some situation with your cousin / –

PRITI. She's my hostage.

GAR. Your what?

PRITI. You heard me.

GAR. What's she worth?

PRITI. Safe passage all weekend. As long as I have her, the 'rents can't tell me shit. And after that, I don't really care.

GAR. What are you even talking about?

PRITI. Hey, I brought a car and a hostage, what did you bring?

LEELA. I brought my journal.

GAR. You didn't give me time to bring anything, I don't even have my phone.

LEELA. And a pen.

GAR. And now my socks are wet.

PRITI. No one cares.

GAR. Which still doesn't explain what she's doing here.

PRITI. I don't need to explain anything to you given that you're "taking some personal space" from our relationship to think your personal space thoughts, I wouldn't want to interrupt that, god, what if you lose your thread?

GAR. What is your problem?

PRITI. She and her mom took my room.

GAR. What?

PRITI. They didn't RSVP or anything, just showed up this morning.

The one thing that was making this whole stupid weekend worth it is that I was going to have my own room at the hotel, and then they gave it away. So I call bullshit!

(Silence. **GAR** *is in disbelief.)*

LEELA. My mother sent an e-mail.

PRITI. To who, to my mom?

LEELA. No, to my father and then we got on a plane.

PRITI. Okay see that's not an actual RSVP.

(Silence.)

GAR. Okay, whatever, all I'm suggesting is that / –

PRITI. What?

GAR. There's a certain lack of privacy in your evil master plan here.

PRITI. You can act like she's not here, she practically doesn't exist anyway.

GAR. God, don't be a jerk.

PRITI. I'm not, it's true, her dad moved them back to Calcutta when she was like five, and it's like she was deleted, I actually forgot she existed. There's like one picture, when they name all the cousins, half the time they forget her, her dad never mentions her, it's like she doesn't exist. So it's extra special great that they gave "nobody" my room. And then they expect me to babysit her? She's freaking seventeen, "Don't let her out of your sight, Priti."

Well there she is, in my sight, and as a special bonus I'm showing her the sights. Yay me.

LEELA. Have you seen the aliens?

PRITI. It's my last weekend before I take off, but do they consider that I might have plans? Hell no! So hostage! You do as I say or there will be consequences, you hear?

LEELA. Yes.

PRITI. S'right. This is my night.

GAR. Okay, I don't need to be here for this.

PRITI. It's our night. We had plans, hasta la vista OC, right? This was our plan.

GAR. Yeah well some of us aren't actually leaving, are we. Some of us got waitlisted. So you and your cousin go ahead and do the list and have a great wedding weekend, I need to go home and dry off.

PRITI. No. We had a plan. I don't quit. No quitters in the OC, 'cause John Wayne's always watching, right?

Listen, you need to do this night with me and stop brooding about shit that won't even matter by this time next year when your life is actually happening and you're away from here.

GAR. Says you.

PRITI. Yeah, says me! Okay you know what, we're done here, I'm checking this off.

GAR. I already said that.

PRITI. But now I said it, and I am in fact the boss of this night, I'm the boss of this whole situation!

GAR. Great.

PRITI. Let's go.

GAR. I'm not in the mood to go.

PRITI. Get in the mood!

GAR. Drive me home!

PRITI. No!

LEELA. Are you two in love?

> *(Beat.)*

PRITI. What?

LEELA. My mother says that sometimes people who love each other fight because they love each other so much.

PRITI. Yeah? That sounds like some parental bullshit.

LEELA. But my grandfather says that sometimes people fight because they don't love each other at all, and some people can't tell the difference.

GAR. Word.

LEELA. We could summon our resources, that's what my mom would do. We can summon the gods for assistance.

PRITI. Can it, hostage. Let's go.

LEELA. If you want to fight aliens instead of each other.

GAR. I'm not fighting.

PRITI. I need some water, this Nutella won't get off my tongue.

GAR. I told you. Are there like spare shoes in the trunk?

PRITI. *(To* **LEELA.***)* Get in back.

GAR. Would you stop snapping at everyone like you're in charge?

PRITI. I am in charge.

LEELA. If you're in love, you'll probably be torn apart. During the war.

GAR. Good, then maybe I'll get some peace.

LEELA. Not really. It's a war.

PRITI. I am in charge! I'm in charge, so everyone sit the hell down, okay?

(*To* **LEELA.**) And you, mellow with the weird shit. If I'm going to watch you I want you to act normal, okay?

LEELA. Okay.

PRITI. Anyone know how to get to Schaffer Park from here?

(*Car starts up, scene transforms to...*)

Scene Six: The Porta-Potty

(**LEELA** *and* **PRITI** *enter, there's a porta-potty.*)

[Illustration: Schaffer Park – a gazebo, fencing, possibly signage, slightly more shading and color than the previous illustration.]

PRITI. That's the toilet.

LEELA. Inside the box?

PRITI. Yeah, inside the box.

GAR. (*Offstage.*) I found it!

PRITI. No way!

(**LEELA** *wiggles the handle of the porta-potty.*)

LEELA. The box is occupied. I'll wait.

(**GAR** *enters with an old, dirty tupperware container, a large one. No shoes.*)

GAR. My mom's probably still looking for this tupperware container. It was her good large one, perfect for bringing samosas.

PRITI. God, I was such a dick.

GAR. You were fine.

PRITI. You should have sold me out.

GAR. It's tupperware, it's not like you stole a kidney. Why would you even say that, I've never sold you out. Ever. Besides, it was worth it.

(**GAR** *cracks open the container, pulls out a kid's baseball mitt and ball.*)

The time capsule that got me out of Little League.

(**PRITI** *pulls out an old retainer.*)

PRITI. And didn't get me out of anything, they just bought me a new retainer and suspended my allowance.

GAR. Like they were going to let their perfect little daughter grow up in America without perfect teeth.

PRITI. Oh god, it still smells like samosas.

GAR. That's wrong.

PRITI. Hey...let's play!

GAR. No...

PRITI. Let's play!

GAR. I took my shoes off...

PRITI. Come on! Leel, do you play baseball?

LEELA. No.

(GAR tries to put on the mitt.)

GAR. I can't even get my hand in this thing.

PRITI. Leel just go in a bush or something, the lock's probably busted.

(PRITI and GAR exit to play catch. The porta-potty door rattles.)

(Beat. Beat.)

LEELA. Hello?

(Offstage "smack" of the ball hitting GAR.)

GAR. *(Offstage.)* Ow!

PRITI. *(Offstage.)* Oh shit, sorry! You used to not be this bad!

GAR. *(Offstage.)* I was always this bad, that's why I quit!

(Door handle rattles again. Beat.)

LEELA. Are you okay?

(Offstage "crack" of the ball knocking over a trash can or something.)

PRITI. *(Offstage.)* You used to be able to catch the ball!

GAR. *(Offstage.)* You used to not be trying to nail me in the head with the ball!

(Rattle, Rattle...)

LEELA. Do you need help? I can get my cousin, she can probably help. Or her boyfriend. But I don't know if they are on or off.

(Rattle, Rattle, Bang.)

PRITI. *(Offstage.)* Okay well back up a bit!

LEELA. I can try to get you out.

PRITI. *(Offstage.)* Little further!

> (**LEELA** *reaches for the door, but from the porta-potty comes a grunt, then a groan.* **LEELA** *reconsiders…*)

LEELA. But my mother told me about a demon trapped by the gods until a human set it free and now it roams the earth and no one has been able to trap it again. So maybe I will not let you out.

> *(Bang. Bang. Bang. Bang. Bang.)*

PRITI. *(Offstage.)* Ready?

GAR. *(Offstage.)* Ready!

PRITI. *(Offstage.)* Okay!

> *(Smash! Sound of breaking glass.)*

Oh shit oh shit oh shit!

LEELA. I think I will not let you out.

> (**PRITI** *sprints across the stage toward the car.*)

PRITI. Leel! Leel, we gotta go!

LEELA. I have not peed yet.

I have not peed yet, and there is a man trapped.

> (**GAR** *runs across the stage toward the car.*)

GAR. Go! Let's go let's go!

LEELA. I think it's a man.

(To the porta-potty.) Are you a man?!

It's hard to tell.

PRITI. *(Offstage.)* Leel, come on!

> (**PRITI** *honks the car horn offstage.*)

LEELA. Yes. Okay.

(To the porta-potty.) I have to go. I have not peed yet, but I can hold it.

> (**LEELA** *runs off. Scene transforms to…*)

Scene Seven: The Billboard

(**PRITI** *and* **LEELA** *tromp through shrubs and bushes. It's dark.*)

[Illustration: A freeway barrier, maybe some green behind it. More complex than the previous drawing.]

PRITI. *(Singing to the melody of "When Johnny Comes Marching Home.")*
"THE ANIMALS WALK IN TWO BY TWO"
...Gaaaar!

LEELA. Which way are we going?

PRITI. Gaaaar!

LEELA. This way?

PRITI. Gar catch up, what the hell?
"THE ANIMALS WALK IN TWO BY TWO, HURRAH,
HURRAH!"

GAR. *(Offstage.)* We left my shoes!

PRITI. What?

GAR. *(Offstage.)* We left my shoes! At the picnic place! I left my shoes at the picnic place!

PRITI. *(Laughs.)* Oh shit.

(**GAR** *enters, shoeless,* **PRITI** *laughs harder.*)

GAR. We have to go back.

PRITI. We're not going back.

GAR. We have to go back, I need my shoes.

PRITI. Well you shouldn't have left them, it's your own fault.

GAR. We're going back to get my shoes! Let's go!

PRITI. What do you think, Leel?

GAR. Who cares what she thinks, let's go!

LEELA. Is it far?

PRITI. Well yeah, it'd be like an hour before we got back here.

GAR. Or we don't bother coming back here and we go home!

LEELA. That's far.

PRITI. It is, right?

GAR. Enough, okay? This isn't funny, let's just go.

LEELA. I don't want to go back.

GAR. No one asked you.

LEELA. She did.

PRITI. Leela has spoken, we're not going back.

GAR. I left my shoes!!

PRITI. Oh calm down, we can get them on the way home, no one's going to steal them.

GAR. I am not walking around without shoes!

PRITI. But you are. You are, I mean no one else here left their shoes behind.

LEELA. If you check yourself before you leave your house you won't forget things.

PRITI. You're the one that took your shoes off.

LEELA. And now you can't find them.

GAR. I don't need to find them, I know where they are, I just need the two of you to get back in the car so we can go get them!

LEELA. And sometimes I count so that I don't forget things.

PRITI. Come on, let's go.

GAR. No!

LEELA. And sometimes I count backwards when I get stuck, and then I get unstuck. You can try counting backwards.

GAR. I'm not stuck, I'm going back.

>   (**GAR** *exits, expecting them to follow. They
>   don't.*)

PRITI. (*To* **LEELA.**) Hey you know there's this one picture of us when we were like three? Well you were two. I should show it to you, we're both in these pink rompers and matching bangles, and / –

LEELA. You're eating my bangle.

PRITI. Yeah...

LEELA. I've seen that picture. My mother thinks it's funny, so she put it on the wall.

PRITI. It's pretty classic, I've got both the bangles in my mouth.

LEELA. And I'm crying.

PRITI. Yeah well you were two.

LEELA. Because you took my bangle.

PRITI. You were crying because you were two, not because I –

LEELA. I was crying because you took my bangle.

PRITI. You don't know that.

LEELA. I do.

PRITI. That's not fair!

LEELA. That's because you took my bangle.

PRITI. Well anyway. It's a classic pic, we're cute as hell.

LEELA. Okay.

(**GAR** *re-enters.*)

GAR. Guys! I'm serious!

PRITI. Dude we're not going back for your shoes.

GAR. Okay, well then give me the keys!

PRITI. No.

GAR. Give me the keys!

PRITI. *(To* **LEELA.***)* You see that billboard over there?

LEELA. Yes.

PRITI. Let's climb!

(*They run.*)

[Illustration (as they arrive at the billboard): Tall power line structure, a sense of height.]

GAR. Wait! Pree!

PRITI. You want the keys, come and get them!

GAR. Stop!

PRITI. Would you please pay attention to where we are? We have arrived, dufus! Item number three!

GAR. It's a billboard.

LEELA. It's the back of a billboard.

GAR. It's just a billboard.

PRITI. Look harder.

LEELA. The picture is on the other side of the billboard.

GAR. Oh. No. No no no no no no way no.

PRITI. Freshman year, you put this on the list.

GAR. No! I was stupid!

PRITI. I'm climbing it, you can do whatever.

GAR. I have no shoes!

PRITI. Friends. Compatriots, County-men. I give you the highest peak in the OC!

LEELA. Santiago Peak.

PRITI. This billboard!

LEELA. That's very inaccurate.

PRITI. It's metaphoric.

LEELA. I don't like metaphors.

GAR. And this is probably illegal!

LEELA. We can go to Santiago Peak.

GAR. Pree, come on, it's high as hell!

PRITI. Welcome to the point.

LEELA. It's lower than Santiago Peak.

(**LEELA** *climbs.*)

GAR. Shit. Pree, your cousin!

PRITI. *(Looking.)* I see that, ass.

GAR. Yeah? You see that? What are you going to do about it?

PRITI. Leela, slow down!

–

I tried.

GAR. Hey kid, just stop halfway, halfway is good!

PRITI. She's only a year younger than we are.

LEELA. We have to climb to the top. It's not a real adventure otherwise.

GAR. Do something!

PRITI. Do what?

LEELA. I'm good at climbing.

>   (**PRITI** *climbs after her.*)

PRITI. Okay, let's go.

GAR. This is so fucking nuts

>   (**GAR** *starts climbing.*)

I hate this.

PRITI. Yeah, look at us! Hey Leel, you ever hear the expression "third wheel"?

LEELA. Like a tricycle?

PRITI. Yeah, like a tricycle... You don't speak English much, do you?

GAR. Slow down!

PRITI. *(Laughs.)* Oh man! You feel that wind?

LEELA. Wind speed increases at higher elevations because there is less friction.

GAR. Wind speed increases is so not okay.

PRITI. *(Hollering.)* Look out, wooooorld!

GAR. Christ, save it for when we get to the top...

LEELA. *(To* **PRITI.***)* Why are you yelling?

PRITI. Just making my presence knoooown!

LEELA. *(To* **GAR.***)* Why is she yelling?

GAR. Because she's nuts.

>   (**LEELA** *arrives at the top, stands, looks out.*
>   *Glow of freeway lights pointing elsewhere.*)

PRITI. *(To* **GAR.***)* You know it would serve you right if I just did the whole list without you!

>   (**PRITI** *arrives at the top.*)

GAR. *(Not breathing okay.)* Okay let's be clear, we made The List when we were kids, and some of us have other shit in our lives now and don't have time for this childish bullshit, but hey thanks so much for your sensitivity and consideration and like the endangerment of life and limb, thanks so much for that!

PRITI. Item number three, beer on the billboard.

(**PRITI** *pulls out a beer.*)

Beer.

(*Hollers.*) Billbooooaaaaard.

(**GAR** *arrives at the top.*)

GAR. I want to see the list. You don't even have it, you're making this shit up.

(**PRITI** *pulls a list out of her back pocket, hands it to* **GAR**.)

"Beer on the billboard." I can't believe you kept this. Fine.

PRITI. Fine.

GAR. Fine.

(**PRITI** *hands* **GAR** *a beer.*)

This is stupid.

PRITI. Sip it slow, don't want you to get a head rush and fall off.

GAR. Shut up.

PRITI. 'Cause it's really far, you should look down. Hey Leel, you want a beer?

GAR. Stop.

PRITI. She's seventeen, and she's a better climber than you are, back off Grandpa. So you want?

LEELA. Okay.

(**PRITI** *hands* **LEELA** *a can,* **LEELA** *opens it, sips, doesn't like it much.*)

PRITI. Look at us. Hanging out. Like 100 feet off the ground. High wind speeds.

(**PRITI** *lies down, looks at the sky, sips beer.*)

GAR. Nothing is okay about this...

(**GAR** *lies down too. A longish silence.*)

God it's so fucking high...

PRITI. Tell me how scared you are...

GAR. It's so fucking high.

PRITI. Tell me in detail...

LEELA. *(Yelling up to the sky.)* Helloooo!!

GAR. Jesus!

> (**LEELA** *waves her arms.*)

LEELA. Hello!

GAR. What are we yelling at?

PRITI. Look at the sky...

> *(They lay there, silence for a bit.)*

GAR. Pree, you realize that this is pointless, right? Whatever you imagined this was going to be, it's not, time passed, we changed.

PRITI. I don't know, this is kind of amazing.

GAR. I mean look at this, *(Re: the list.)* the candy lady doesn't even live there anymore, she moved to Alaska like three years ago.

PRITI. See it's this kind of negative attitude that keeps you on the ground instead of on top of a billboard.

GAR. I mean where did you even keep this, like in a box under your bed tied with a ribbon? With your name written on it in pink with flowers wittle hearts dotting the i's, with your pink gel pen?

PRITI. I'm gonna explore our peak. You try not to fall off.

> (**PRITI** *climbs away to explore more billboard.*)

GAR. *(Calling.)* Explore what? Explore where? This thing is like thirty feet across, where are you going?

> (**PRITI** *doesn't respond.* **GAR** *stares after her.*)

I can't even. What am I doing here, this is so stupid. So, so stupid.

LEELA. Can I see your list?

> (**GAR** *hands her the list.*)

GAR. Keep it. Can I see yours?

>   (**LEELA** *hands* **GAR** *her journal, he glances through.*)

Nice. Um.

So...

You live in India?

LEELA. Yes.

GAR. Dope. And um...what do you do there?

LEELA. We have school at home.

GAR. Ah man, home-schooled, no wonder.

No, it's just...home-schooled kids, they're a thing. It's like they're chicklets or something, little hatchling creatures with like fuzz and their eyes are all glazy and blind and never seen the sun.

So you like it?

LEELA. It's okay. I can't be by myself.

GAR. Why's that?

LEELA. I have bad judgement.

GAR. Well in that case they shouldn't let Pree be by herself either.

>   (**LEELA** *smiles.*)

You like it up here?

LEELA. Yes.

GAR. I'm terrified.

LEELA. It's okay. Nothing bad will happen.

GAR. Yeah okay. Thanks.

LEELA. *(To the sky.)* Summoning all Gods! Are you up there?

GAR. Sound probably carries like crazy from up here, you keep telling them.

LEELA. Come down now! We need assistance!

GAR. Yeah we do! We're on a freaking billboard.

LEELA. I'll write them a message.

GAR. Good idea.

(**LEELA** *writes a message on the back of the list:*)

LEELA. "Hello Gods. The humans need your assistance. Please come now. Love, Leela."

(**LEELA** *folds the paper into a paper airplane.*)

GAR. That's good, that's clear, to the point.

(**LEELA** *throws the paper airplane, it flies off, they watch. Airplane hum from beginning rises loud.*)

LEELA. Ladies and gentlemen, we are now cleared for flying, the temperature on Mount Meru is very cold because it is the top of a mountain and gods can't feel cold anyway.

(**PRITI** *re-enters.*)

PRITI. Was that my list?

GAR. Yup.

PRITI. What the hell?

LEELA. Sorry.

GAR. Say bye bye.

PRITI. We're not going back for your shoes.

GAR. I'll cry about that just as soon as I finish dealing with my actual real-world problems.

PRITI. Really? So now you don't care?

GAR. It doesn't even matter. You're leaving Monday, and once you leave Orange you're for damn sure not coming back.

PRITI. Jealous?

GAR. No. I'm not jealous, I'm just not going anywhere. So this little send-off is all about you. Like everything else.

PRITI. Wow.

LEELA. Did they receive the message?

GAR. I don't know. Have they replied?

LEELA. I don't see anything.

PRITI. That's Orange County, nothing as far as the eye can see. And my mom can't believe I want to leave.

GAR. Yeah, well she was made for this place. Except she can't swim, that part's weird.

PRITI. "It is paradise on earth, Priti, why would you want to leave?"

GAR. God, we have to climb down too.

PRITI. Stop thinking about it. Just *be* here.

GAR. Thank you, Yoda.

PRITI. It'll be fine, we'll get down, right now just *be* here. Look at us. We're on top of the billboard.

GAR. JR dared me to climb it.

PRITI. What?

GAR. When I was like ten, remember JR, he lived like two blocks over and had that stick? He was always daring people and like pointing it everywhere. He dared me to climb this billboard, and I cried and like peed my pants, it was awful, that's why I put it on the list.

PRITI. We can call him when we get down.

GAR. I don't know where he is anymore.

PRITI. Maybe he's in Alaska too.

GAR. Maybe. But okay. Item checked off. Thanks.

PRITI. You're welcome.

LEELA. *(Hollering.)* Gods! Did you get my message?!

(A moment. Then **GAR** *gets on board.)*

GAR. *(Hollering.)* Yeah! We sent you a letter! From the edge!

PRITI. *(Hollering.)* Of a billboard!

LEELA. Save the humans!

PRITI. Yeah, the humans! And like the trees! And the whales!

GAR. I don't really care about the whales, that's not a deal-breaker!

(Fireworks "boom" in the distance, **GAR** *freaks out, sits, shaking.)*

Jesus, shit! I'm not going to survive this night, seriously!

PRITI. Hey Leel, I think they're answering!

LEELA. What is that?

PRITI. Disneyland, baby! Them's our California gods,
("Johnny Comes Marching Home" melody.)
"THE PRINCESSES GO IN TWO BY TWO, HURRAH,
   HURRAH."

LEELA. The Gods.

GAR. They actually match up kind of perfectly.

PRITI. Like Seeta and Rama are like Beauty and the Beast,
except if what's his name.

GAR. Gaston.

PRITI. Yeah if Gaston was her true love and actually rescued
her...

GAR. And Hanuman is like Mickey Mouse.

PRITI. And the dwarves all have names like "sensible."

GAR. "Attractive," "highly intelligent"...

PRITI. "Go-getter."

GAR. "Valedictorian."

PRITI. "Marriageable."

GAR. "Loser."

　　　　　*(**PRITI** looks at **GAR**.)*

I'm kidding, calm down.

PRITI. We claim this billboard for the Indian aunties! May
they forever rule this paradise. But we're getting out!
We're getting out, you hear me!

LEELA. I think those are fireworks.

　　　　　*(Sound of fireworks rises. Scene transforms
　　　　　to...)*

Scene Eight: The India Mart

(A supermarket. Musak* plays. **LEELA** *looks at a rack of oranges, draws.)*

[Illustration: A rectangle with long legs, below it a rack of oranges. On the rectangle is a sign with a price: "$3.99/lb." This is a detailed drawing, the oranges are orange.]

(A **GIRL** *of about nine walks up, sucking on a juice box, watches* **LEELA**. **LEELA** *stares back.)*

GIRL. They're from Florida.

LEELA. Who?

GIRL. The oranges are from Florida. See, it says on them. Flo-ri-da Oranges.

LEELA. Okay.

GIRL. They've traveled.

> *(Beat.* **GAR** *zooms by on an empty shopping cart.)*

GAR. ...And he clears the corner with seconds to spare, but will he make it past the finish line in time, oh NOOOO! CURSE YOU, CAMPBELL'S SOOUUUUUUPPPPP!!

> *(***GAR***'s gone. Musak*.)*

GIRL. Is he with you?

LEELA. With my cousin.

GIRL. Where's your cousin?

LEELA. Here. Somewhere.

GIRL. Are you with your cousin too?

LEELA. Yes.

GIRL. So you're here all together? The three of you?

LEELA. Yes.

GIRL. Then he's with you too. Not just with your cousin. Because you're all together.

LEELA. Okay.

> *(Musak*. Silence. They observe the Florida oranges. The* **GIRL** *notices* **LEELA**'s *journal.)*

GIRL. What's that?

LEELA. My journal.

GIRL. Can I see it?

> **(LEELA** *hands it over,* **GIRL** *looks.)*

Why is the first page empty?

LEELA. Clouds.

GIRL. Huh?

LEELA. Clouds. From the plane.

GIRL. You didn't draw anything.

LEELA. Clouds are white.

GIRL. It's not a drawing if you don't draw anything. It's just a piece of paper.

LEELA. I don't think so.

GIRL. It's true. You have to make it so people can see what it is. That's the point of drawing. You can't just leave it blank.

> *(No comment from* **LEELA**.*)*

When I draw clouds, I do them like this:

> **(GIRL** *demonstrates helpfully in air, a big puffy air-cloud.)*

Like that. That's how you draw a cloud.

LEELA. No. Clouds don't look like that.

GIRL. They do.

---

*A license to produce *Orange* does not include a performance license for any third-party or copyrighted music. Licensees should create an original composition or use music in the public domain. For further information, please see Music Use Note on page 3.

LEELA. They don't.

GIRL. They do.

    I'm really good at drawing.

LEELA. I'm really good at drawing.

GIRL. You didn't draw anything!

LEELA. Have you looked at clouds?

GIRL. I draw clouds a lot.

LEELA. Maybe you're bad at looking.

GIRL. You can't draw nothing and say it's something.

LEELA. Why not?

GIRL. Because no one knows what it is!

LEELA. I know what it is.

GIRL'S DAD. *(Offstage.)* Lily! We're done!

        (**GIRL** *turns the page.*)

GIRL. What's this one.

LEELA. It's an orange.

GIRL. It's a circle.

GIRL'S DAD. *(Offstage.)* Lily!

GIRL. That's not how you draw.

        (**LEELA** *pulls the orange her dad gave her out of her pocket, shows it to* **GIRL**. *Clearly circular.*)

LEELA. It's an orange.

GIRL. Why do you have that in your pocket? You can't take that.

LEELA. Yes.

GIRL. You can't put it in your pocket, you can put it in a basket or a cart, but not in your pocket. That's the law.

LEELA. My dad gave it to me.

GIRL. Well he has to pay for it, did he pay for it?

LEELA. He gave it to me.

GIRL. Put it back.

LEELA. Why?

GIRL. Put it back.

LEELA. No.

GIRL'S DAD. *(Offstage.)* Lily! Now!

GIRL. Put it back, or I'll tell!

LEELA. No!

GIRL'S DAD. *(Offstage.)* Lily!

GIRL. DAAAD! She's stealing! Dad!

LEELA. I'm not.

(**GIRL** *runs offstage as* **GAR** *re-enters.*)

GAR. Pree's done, let's jet.

GIRL. *(Offstage.)* She's stealing she's stealing!

GAR. What the hell?

LEELA. It's mine.

GIRL. *(Offstage.)* She's stealing, Dad!

GAR. What?

LEELA. It's my orange.

GAR. Look, I don't have my wallet, so unless you got cash...

LEELA. It's mine.

GAR. Just put it back and let's get out of here.

GIRL. *(Offstage.)* She's stealing!

LEELA. It's mine!

GAR. Just...we'll get another one, look they're getting the store manager, let's just go!

(**GAR** *grabs at the orange.*)

LEELA.	**GAR.**
It's mine! Mine! Mine! Mine! Mine!	Shut up! Pipe the hell down!
(They wrestle over it.)	
It's mine! It's mine! It's mine! It's mine!	Give it to me! Just! Stop! They're looking right at us, I can't! Shit! What can I do to get you to let the fuck go of this orange? Name it, okay?

LEELA.	GAR.
IT'S MINE MINE MINE MINE MINE MINE MINE MINE MINE MINE...	Name it! Just say what you want, say it fast, 'cause we need to get out of here! We're gonna get in trouble. C'mon, please. Look, just go outside, go outside and I'll go find Pree and meet you. Okay? Just wait outside. Wait outside wait outside wait outside, jesus, what is wrong with you?

FEMALE STORE MANAGER. *(Offstage.)* Hey! Hey you!

> (**LEELA** *loses her grip on the orange,* **GAR** *takes it from her. Musak* rises, loud, menacing...*)

LEELA. NOOOOO! NO NO NO NO!

GAR. Kid!

LEELA. IT'S MINE! MINE!

> (*Musak* is really loud now, it's kind of awful.*)

Go away go away go away count to ten count to ten count to ten oranges hanging on a tree, One fell down and that makes nine oranges hanging on a tree, One fell down and that makes eight oranges hanging on a tree...

> (**GAR** *is farther and farther away.*)

GAR. *(Offstage.)* Leela! Wait!

> (**LEELA** *continues under her breath, runs from the supermarket, leaving* **GAR** *behind.*)

---

*A license to produce *Orange* does not include a performance license for any third-party or copyrighted music. Licensees should create an original composition or use music in the public domain. For further information, please see Music Use Note on page 3.

LEELA. Seven oranges, hanging on a tree, one fell...makes six oranges...hanging on a...tree...and that makes five... oranges...

> (**LEELA** *is alone, running.*)

Hanging on a tree, one...and that makes four oranges hanging on a tree...and that makes three oranges hanging on a tree, one fell down and that makes...two oranges hanging from a tree, one...

It's okay now... It's okay it's okay it's okay...

I don't know where I am...

> (*Scene transforms to...*)

Scene Nine: The Orange Tree

(The Orange Tree.)

[Illustration: A gorgeous and ornate orange tree slowly spreads across the backdrop. The oranges have an almost mystical quality.]

(LEELA stares at it. An OLD DUDE sleeping up against the trunk wakes, peers at LEELA.)

OLD DUDE. No squatting.

LEELA. What?

OLD DUDE. This here's an aesthetic choice. The Tree. So no squatting.

LEELA. I'm not.

OLD DUDE. Oh. My mistake then. You been standing there a while, staring and mumbling to yourself. What's so interesting?

LEELA. The oranges. They're real.

OLD DUDE. Yeah, but don't eat 'em, they're probably not sprayed or something.

LEELA. Okay.

OLD DUDE. I'm serious.

LEELA. Okay.

I had an orange.

OLD DUDE. Good for you. Vitamin C.

LEELA. My father gave it to me.

OLD DUDE. S'nice.

LEELA. But I couldn't hold it. It's gone.

OLD DUDE. Happens.

LEELA. I can't go back to the supermarket. It's not safe.

OLD DUDE. Yeah, they don't let me in neither.

LEELA. I like this tree.

OLD DUDE. Me too. Best place to sleep.

They used to be everywhere. The trees. Paradise on earth. You're about seventy-five years late.

LEELA. For what?

OLD DUDE. Humans. Trimmed and clipped it down to this...this nub...one perfectly manicured tree, and a town named Orange. Shame. Shame on the humans.

LEELA. Why didn't the gods stop them?

OLD DUDE. The gods. Now they never should have given us the keys to the place. Once we moved in, it was only a matter of time 'til we forced them out.

People don't live in multi-generational households no more, now everything's all nuclear. Only a matter of time before the spirits moved out of the cupboards and the trees. The gods don't get too involved these days. They leave us to our mess.

LEELA. So they're not here?

OLD DUDE. No one here but me.

(*Pause.* **LEELA** *eyes* **OLD DUDE** *suspiciously.*)

LEELA. What are *you* doing here?

OLD DUDE. Warning people off the oranges. They're not sprayed. What are *you* doing here?

LEELA. I need help.

OLD DUDE. That so. What sort of help?

LEELA. My mother needs resources. For the battle.

PRITI. (*Offstage.*) Leel! Leel!

LEELA. So I'm searching for the gods. But I can't find them.

PRITI. (*Offstage.*) Get away from him! What the hell!

OLD DUDE. Who's that?

LEELA. My cousin.

OLD DUDE. She's loud.

LEELA. Yes.

(**PRITI** *enters, running, carrying a brown paper bag.*)

PRITI. Leel! What the hell, you can't just run off like that!

LEELA. I'm her hostage.

PRITI. You're a shitty hostage, you need a damn keeper! C'mon, Gar's waiting.

LEELA. Gar is her boyfriend. He took my orange.

OLD DUDE. Well that's not right.

PRITI. Listen I'm done, I got the things, let's just get back to the car.

OLD DUDE. Oh, no, no, no, no.

PRITI. Who *are* you?

OLD DUDE. Don't let 'em hem you in. To a car. You got places to be.

PRITI. Okay, you're really not invited to this conversation.

OLD DUDE. Outside that vehicular contrivance. Outside of where that vehicular contrivance can transport you.

PRITI. Don't talk to him, let's go.

OLD DUDE. Car limits a person. To a road.

PRITI. Let's go, Leel! Jesus, Gar's right, you can't be alone...

OLD DUDE. Unless it's an off-road vehicle. But still the options are limited to areas traversable on ground.

PRITI. ...Walk away from the crazy guy.

OLD DUDE. And you don't want that. Don't want to be limited to the ground. Nuh-uh, no way, no Jose, no nobody.

PRITI. Who the hell is this freak??

LEELA. He guards the tree.

OLD DUDE. Now a surf board. A surf board don't limit a man.

PRITI. What?

OLD DUDE. Surf.

PRITI. Yeah, well, ocean's that way, old guy.

OLD DUDE. Old Dude. I prefer Dude. And yeah, can't go, can't go to no ocean.

LEELA. Why?

OLD DUDE. Got no legs. No legs, no surfing, no more.

> *(He shows. Oh hell.)*

PRITI. How do you...? Where's your wheelchair?

OLD DUDE. Oh I get around, don't you worry. Go on now. Ocean's where you want to be.

LEELA. Okay.

PRITI. C'mon, let's go.

>*(Beat.)*

LEELA. *(To* **OLD DUDE.***)* Are you a prophet?

OLD DUDE. Nah.

LEELA. Can you get a message to the gods?

OLD DUDE. Ha! I look mobile to you?

LEELA. Give them a message. We need them.

OLD DUDE. Give them a message? Give them a message?

>**(OLD DUDE** *is suddenly less friendly, he's kinda scary, now he's just a crazy dude on the street.)*

Have you seen my legs? Because I haven't! No way, no Jose, No Nowhere! They abandoned me! The Gods, they abandoned me! I can't find them Nowhere!

PRITI. Oh shit...you stay away from her!

OLD DUDE. Give them a message??

PRITI. Stay away! Come on, Leel. Come on, let's go! Come on!

OLD DUDE. Hey kid! Be careful out there.

>**(OLD DUDE** *laughs and laughs.* **PRITI** *grabs* **LEELA** *and drags her off. Honking of cars. Scene transforms to...)*

Scene Ten: The Parking Lot

(In the parking lot. **LEELA** *sits in the car.* **PRITI** *glares at* **GAR**, *who is offstage. He has her phone and her keys.)*

[Illustration: Strip mall parking lot, buildings, street lights.]

PRITI. Gar!

GAR. *(Offstage.)* No!

PRITI. Give them!

GAR. *(Offstage.)* No!

     (**PRITI** *darts at* **GAR**, *he enters countering her move and staying out of reach, keeps the car between them.)*

PRITI. Hand them over right now!

GAR. No! You've got like twenty-seven missed calls here, it's like your entire family!

PRITI. Give me my phone, and get in the car!

GAR. *(Reading.)* "Call immediately," "Is Leela with you?" What the hell Pree?

PRITI. Give me my damn phone!

GAR. No! You need to get off your megalo-trip and get this kid back to her parents!

PRITI. Why are you such an epic loser?

GAR. Because I'm on the freaking sugarland express with you, and I'll probably end up in jail! Also, she is not okay, she needs to go home!

PRITI. Leel! You want to go back to your parents?

LEELA. I want to go to the ocean.

PRITI. She wants to go to the beach!

GAR. Just get in the passenger side, I'll drive her back.

PRITI. It's my car!

GAR. It's your sister's, and I'm pretty sure she'd back me on this one! Get in the passenger side!

PRITI. You don't even have a wallet!

GAR. You don't have a moral compass!

PRITI. Okay I've got Leela back! She's fine, she's found, she's here! I won't let her out of my sight again, okay? But I'm not going back, we're not finished, it's barely freaking eleven! I'll have her back by midnight, this is the night, come on, it'll never be this night again, how can you want to just end it?

GAR. Because I'm not having a good time! Because I never wanted to start it!

LEELA. I'm having a good time.

PRITI. I mean you're awfully fucking sanguine about this... you don't think however many fucking years we've been together deserves some kind of send-off?

GAR. Yeah except we weren't actually together, so I'm finding it pretty easy to move on from our non-relationship.

(*Beat.*)

PRITI. Fine, I'll drive you home.

GAR. Yeah?

PRITI. Yeah, that's what you want.

GAR. Okay. And the kid?

(**PRITI** *takes the keys from* **GAR.**)

PRITI. I thought you were in love with me.

GAR. Yeah well. Things change. Let's go.

(*Scene transforms to...*)

Scene Eleven: The Pacific Coast Highway

(**PRITI** *drives very fast down the PCH,* **GAR** *in the passenger seat,* **LEELA** *in back.*)

[Illustration: Dots like manic stars scatter around.]

GAR. Dammiiiiiitttttt, that was our exit!! Pree!

PRITI. What?

GAR. You didn't see her back there, she needs to go home! Take her home!

PRITI. I don't feel like it, so back the hell off! Besides Leel wants to go to the beach!

LEELA. I do.

GAR. That's not a decision she should be making, she is not okay!

PRITI. Hey Leel, you okay?

LEELA. Yes.

PRITI. Yeah so Gar you should shut up. Leel and I got plans.

GAR. I'm done with you, I want to go home.

PRITI. Well I'm not done with you!
You know what, fuck it. Give me this!

(**PRITI** *grabs at* **GAR**.)

GAR. Get off!

PRITI. Give me this.

(**PRITI** *grabs at* **GAR**'s *shirt.*)

GAR. My shirt?

PRITI. It's mine! This is all mine! I mean you don't need it, you're just going to quit everything anyway.

GAR. Get off me!

PRITI. You're just going to stop, like you stopped applying for colleges, and you stopped your endlessly fucking tiresome hitting on me, but that's how I know you're over, you're done, give it to me!

GAR. Get off my shirt!

LEELA. Are you two breaking up now?

> *(He rips his shirt away.)*

PRITI. You don't want me to! You want me on you, pushing you, 'cause otherwise you just sit there!

LEELA. Or are you still in love?

GAR. Damn it Pree, you're fucking up my shirt, and I don't want a damn thing from you!

PRITI. Fine, let's fight, you want to fight?

GAR. No, I don't want to fight, I don't want to fight with you, I don't want to fight.

PRITI. Well I do!

GAR. Why don't you watch the damn road!

LEELA. I like the stars.

PRITI. Fine! I'm over you, *(to* **LEELA.***)* I'm over him! I'm done. I'm done!

You ready for a real adventure, Leel?

LEELA. Yes.

PRITI. Lights out!

GAR. No!

> *(Headlights go out. Spotlight on **LEELA**, she tunes out the screeching screaming sounds of **GAR** and **PRITI** and the car. She beams into the sky, happy.)*

LEELA. Adventures are not airplanes and hotel rooms. Adventures are when you go somewhere different and things happen. Adventures can be dangerous. Adventures are like right now.

> *(Lights back to normal, screeching tires.)*

PRITI. Oh shit oh shit oh shit.

GAR. Stop, stop the car!

> *(Car crashes to a halt in a sand dune. **PRITI** and **GAR** are both mad, crying, and freaked.)*

Okay, great, we're here, look a sand dune, good job. You're unreal!

PRITI. Stop it!

GAR. No you stop, I...

PRITI. I wasn't trying to run into it!

GAR. But you did, didn't you?

PRITI. Stop yelling at me!

GAR. Why? 'Cause you might crash?

PRITI. I just...you...

> (**PRITI** *climbs on top of* **GAR** *and kisses him, long and deep.*)

GAR. What the hell are you... Really?

> (*She kisses him.*)

God, okay stop it, Pree, I don't think this is hot! I mean maybe you think guys like this, but we don't...

PRITI. Don't, don't cry.

GAR. Shit, I mean Christ, have I not been trying to get in your pants all freaking year? I'm not, you've just, you've got me all beaten down with like lack of logic and I'm tired and you almost killed us all, I'm not crying I'm having a freaking biological reaction.

> (**PRITI** *kisses him.*)

Okay, so what, is this a pity thing, 'cause I'm like above it. I mean I wouldn't have thought I would be, but I'm definitely above it.

PRITI. It's not pity.

GAR. Then why couldn't you have made out with me like before I was crying and shit, like four months ago, or even four hours ago, 'cause the timing here –

> (**PRITI** *kisses him.*)

Stop.

> (**PRITI** *kisses him.*)

Quit it.

> (**PRITI** *kisses him.*)

Fine, don't stop. You're making me cry. Not my parents, or college, or that I got rejected by the Starbucks which

I didn't even know was possible. You. Is that what you want? That's what you're after?

PRITI. Yes. It means you care about me.

GAR. Well that's messed up.

PRITI. I know.

> *(They kiss. For a really long time.* **LEELA** *watches patiently. Then...)*

LEELA. Is this the beach?

—

It's dark.

> *(***LEELA** *leans through* **GAR** *and* **PRITI** *and turns on the headlights, illuminating an expanse of sand. Sounds in the distance,* **LEELA** *listens.)*

There's something happening over there.

> *(No response from* **GAR** *and* **PRITI***.)*

Okay.

> *(***LEELA** *exits car. Scene transforms to...)*

Scene Twelve: The Beach

(Sounds of battle offstage. **LEELA** *follows the sounds. Firelight, drunk voices, screams, thumping dark music*, sound of motorcycles, danger. As* **LEELA** *approaches the sounds get closer.)*

[Illustration: Long stretch of beach and night sky.]

WOMAN. *(Offstage.)* It's a damn tree, you're gonna get crushed.

> *(The drunk* **WOMAN** *trips, falls, laughs, onstage.)*

Aaaaaah shit, it's gonna tip!

MAN. *(Offstage.)* Flame on! Get back here, help out!

WOMAN. No no no hell no, I'm not getting near that thing! TIMBER!! Unsafe assholes!

LEELA. What are they burning?

WOMAN. *(Startled.)* Hey. What the fuck. This section of the beach is taken, move on.

LEELA. That's a tree.

WOMAN. It's a sacrifice.

LEELA. Why?

MAN. *(Offstage.)* God damn shit!

> *(Drunk* **MAN** *enters.)*

FIRE!! You like that? Watch it burn!

WOMAN. It's leaning, you need to push it all the way in.

MAN. Oh yeah? That's how you like it, all the way in?

> *(**MAN** grabs **WOMAN***'s ass, she grins.)*

---

*A license to produce *Orange* does not include a performance license for any third-party or copyrighted music. Licensees should create an original composition or use music in the public domain. For further information, please see Music Use Note on page 3.

WOMAN. Hands off, Ricky's watching.

MAN. Good.

WOMAN. Oh you're trying to get in a fight now?

LEELA. Don't touch her!

      (Beat.)

MAN. Who the hell is this?

WOMAN. I don't know.

MAN. Hey, it's a big beach, walk pretty much anywhere but here.

LEELA. No.

MAN. "No."

WOMAN. Just go home, okay?

LEELA. I'll help you.

WOMAN. You'll what? She'll what?

MAN. *(Laughing.)* Where the hell'd you find her? Your mom send her?

WOMAN. Go home, you're not invited to this party.
(To offstage party.) Burn that fucking wood!

MAN. Hey now, you're being inhospitable, buttercup.

WOMAN. I'm trying.

MAN. Maybe she's just thirsty, you want a drink? Sweetpea, get this little girl a beer.

WOMAN. Watch it with the fucking flower names.

MAN. Aww, what, honeysuckle getting mad?

      *(**MAN** and **WOMAN** wrestle down to the sand; it's violent, but it's definitely foreplay. Not to **LEELA** though, to **LEELA** it's battle. Offstage voices: "Fight! Fight! Fight! Fight!")*

LEELA. *(Under her breath.)* Bad man, bad man, bad man, bad man...
(Loudly.) Stop it!

WOMAN. Get off me!

LEELA. Stop!

WOMAN. Get off me!

MAN. Make me.

LEELA. Do you want him to stop?!

WOMAN. Hell yes, get off!

LEELA. Let go of her!

> (**LEELA** *jumps on* **MAN**, *trying to pull him off* **WOMAN**.)

MAN. What the –? Get the fuck off!

WOMAN. Get away, bitch.

MAN. You want in on the foreplay, huh?

LEELA. Don't touch her!

MAN. Or what?

WOMAN. Leave her, Jerry.

LEELA. *(To* **WOMAN**.*)* Stand behind me!

MAN. S'bullshit...

> (**MAN** *exits back to the party.*)

WOMAN. *(To* **LEELA**.*)* Get the hell away, freak.

LEELA. I'm not a freak.

WOMAN. *(To* **LEELA**.*)* Get the fuck away, this party's not for you!

LEELA. No.

WOMAN. Get away! Shoo!

> (**WOMAN** *throws sand at* **LEELA**'s *legs, she recoils.*)

LEELA. I'm trying to help you.

WOMAN. I don't need help! You need help, you got problems, *(Points to head.)* up here...

> (**LEELA** *scrambles away but doesn't leave.*)

And stay away! Fucking...

(To the offstage party.) Push it all the way in, come on! Watch it Burn!

> (**WOMAN** *exits back to the bonfire party.*)

LEELA. I'm watching you.

(*Someone throws a bottle at* **LEELA**, *then someone throws a cup. She dodges, climbs up the sand bank, waits.*)

MAN. (*Offstage, laughing.*) She's still there!

(*Laughter.* **LEELA** *watches, firelight and shadows on her face. Party continues, occasionally* **MAN** *or* **WOMAN** *tip into view, then disappear again.*)

(*Lights and party fade...then lights fade up again. Time has passed.*)

(*Only* **MAN** *is stumbling around now, dropping to the sand, drunk but still conscious, the rest of the party is passed out snoring.*)

Hey...make yourself useful, get me another beer.

(*He laughs.* **LEELA** *doesn't respond.*)

I mean you're still here, so you must want to party. These assholes can't hold their liquor, I need to get better friends. I bet you can hold your liquor.

(*Noticing the bottle.*)

Hey, is there anything left in that bottle? That bottle, right there, it's right by you...

(**LEELA** *doesn't look at the bottle at her feet, keeps watching* **MAN.**)

Come on, bring it over. I'll share. We can have a drink. Bring your pretty face over here. What, you don't trust me?

(**LEELA** *picks up the bottle and draws a half circle in the sand between her and* **MAN.**)

LEELA. Sometimes demons trick you to come outside the circle where you are safe.

MAN. You want me to come get you? That's the kind of girl you are? You want me to come get you? From inside your circle, your... (*Laughs.*) Where you're safe, your sand circle, ha...

> (*He crawls toward her.*)
>
> (**LEELA** *holds the bottle like a weapon in front of her.*)

Here, give me that! Give me that.

> (**LEELA** *suddenly starts yelling, loud, very loud.*)

LEELA. YOU ARE A BAD MAN, THIS IS A BAD MAN, YOU ARE A BAD MAN, GET AWAY FROM ME GET AWAY FROM ME THIS IS A BAD MAN I NEED ASSISTANCE, I NEED ASSISTANCE, GODS! GODS! HELP!

MAN. Shut up, god dammit...

LEELA. GODS! GODS!

> (**MAN** *grabs at* **LEELA**, *she snatches away.*)

MAN. Get over here!

> (**MAN** *comes after her in earnest.*)

LEELA. NO! NO NO NO NO NO! I NEED ASSISTANCE! I NEED ASSISTANCE!

MAN. Stop kicking!!

LEELA. NO!

> (**MAN** *manages to get a grip on* **LEELA**.)

MAN. Got you!

LEELA. NO! WHACHAAH! WHACHAAH!

> (**LEELA** *kicks at him and it's surprisingly effective, he's knocked down, struggling...*)

Sometimes people who fight should not be together. Sometimes people who are bad should stop talking.

> (**LEELA** *paces, doesn't know what to do...*)

The Gods are not coming. The Gods are not coming to help.

Okay. I will help you to stop talking.

(**LEELA** *scoops up sand in the cup, approaches* **MAN** *still struggling on the ground, pours sand in* **MAN**'s *mouth. A choking, sputtering roar of rage from* **MAN**.)

Uh-oh. Uh-oh.

(**MAN** *roars, rises from the sand.*)

(**LEELA** *runs away very, very fast.*)

Six demons sleeping on the beach, One ate sand and that makes five! Five demons sleeping on the beach...

(*Sound of ocean rises,* **MAN** *screams incoherently after her, the sound is like demons shrieking, gradually the battle recedes...*)

Run! Run! Run!

Four demons sleeping on the beach...

(*The sound of yelling is almost gone.*)

Run! Run...

Three demons...

Two demons...

One demon...

Marine layer comes in and that makes...

(*Sound of ocean recedes.* **LEELA** *stops, looks behind her, no one is following, the sounds of the demons and* **MAN** *screaming are gone. Nothing but beach.*)

None.

(*Silence. Wind. Deep gasping breaths.* **LEELA** *straightens up, looks around. She's freezing, shaking.*)

I don't know where I am...

I don't know where I am...

Where am I...

(*A beat. Then, from offstage...*)

PRITI. (*Offstage.*) Leela! Leela!

LEELA. *(Under her breath.)* Priti...

PRITI. *(Offstage.)* Leela!

LEELA. Priti!

> (**PRITI** *enters, panicked, searching. They find each other.*)

PRITI. Leela! Where the hell have you been? God, this fog!

LEELA. It's the marine layer.

PRITI. Jesus!

> (**PRITI** *hugs* **LEELA** *really, really hard.*)

Jesus hell, where have you been? Are you hurt? Tell me if you're hurt, do you understand me, I need a normal person answer, you've been gone for freaking hours!

LEELA. The cool water meets the warm air and makes a fog. It'll burn off by mid-morning.

PRITI. Well thanks for the informative lowdown, now answer the damn question!

LEELA. I am not hurt.

There was a bad man, but I poured sand in his big open mouth and then I ran fast. He is hurt, not me.

PRITI. Oh shit. Oh thank god.

LEELA. No. They didn't come.

PRITI. What?

LEELA. The gods did not come. There was a fight, but they did not come. My mother said that when things are bad that they will come. Like in the stories. But they didn't.

PRITI. Okay. I have no clue what you're talking about, but you're not hurt, so that's... You're freezing... Gar!

GAR. *(Offstage.)* Did you find her?

PRITI. I got her, bring your sweater!

LEELA. *(Teeth chattering.)* I tried to summon them. I tried everything. I called. I sent messages. It didn't work. It didn't work. They didn't come. They didn't bring assistance.

PRITI. Okay, here, sit with me, come on, body heat...

(GAR enters with a sweater. They wrap it around LEELA.)

GAR. Man, kid, where'd you go?

LEELA. The gods didn't come.

PRITI. She had an adventure, she's okay. She's tough, took out some guy who was messing with her. Jesus, I'm freaked, deep breaths everyone, let's just sit here for a second... Where the hell is my phone?

GAR. I'll find it.

(GAR exits.)

PRITI. Deep breaths.

LEELA. My mother wanted to summon our resources.

PRITI. What?

LEELA. That's why we came here. Because my grandfather died. We came here to summon my father. To be with us.

PRITI. Oh... I'm sorry...

LEELA. Because he's too busy to come to Calcutta. And too busy to answer his telephone. And then we got on an airplane. Because my mother was sad. Because my mother needs help. Because I cannot be alone. Do you think he'll come with us?

PRITI. I don't know. So do you guys speak English at home, in Calcutta?

LEELA. Yes. Mother and Grandfather insisted. For when I come to Orange County.

PRITI. Yeah. I thought maybe it was like...maybe a second language. Just...the way you say things sometimes, it's like...I don't know, unique... But your English is really good.

LEELA. Thanks. Look at the sun.

(They look as the light changes.)

[Illustration: A circle, turning orange.]

PRITI. Sunrise. Pretty amazing. Okay...you're safe...okay.

LEELA. Are you crying again?

PRITI. No, just…this is good, you know? It feels good. To be here. I mean you're alive, so that's huge. And it's morning. And… I don't know… I should have grabbed food, I didn't plan, I didn't think we'd be out this late… this early…

LEELA. You didn't finish your list.

PRITI. No. God, look at that sun.

LEELA. It's orange.

PRITI. The beach at dawn. It's good lighting.

A girl's gotta think about these things. When we get older, we can't be hanging out in the morning light, we'll be all chasing down candlelit dinners and dark corners

LEELA. Why?

PRITI. Beauty, baby. It's all about beauty.

I mean it's not, and I'm not all shallow, just, you know, parts. Parts of me are shallow, but I mean that's just an entry point, right, I get deeper the further in you go. Just, I mean, a girl can't be a straight drop-off the cliff and drown type ledge or no one will go swimming, you know?

This metaphor is gross.

Look at you, I'm a mess and you've been up all night and look no different. And you're perfectly lit. And I don't hate you at all. Oh shit. I'm so tired, I'm stupid, oh man, my eyes! What are we doing, Leel??

LEELA. I don't know.

(Looking out over the water.) What's that?

PRITI. Aw, lookit, the dawn surfers…yeah, boy.

LEELA. They're coming?

PRITI. Yup. That they are.

LEELA. The gods are coming?

PRITI. Ha! It's the bros, honey, don't give them any more helium for their egos, k? Pretty sight, though.

*(**GAR** enters, hands **PRITI** her phone.)*

GAR. Your phone's dead.

PRITI. Figures. Leel's got a thing for the surfers.

LEELA. They came.

GAR. Good waves this morning.

PRITI. I mean no joke, Leel, they're hot. Maybe a little old for you.

> (**LEELA** *watches as surfers head off to various vehicles to strip off wetsuits.*)

LEELA. What are they doing?

PRITI. Peeling off their wetsuits. I mean they could go someplace private, but then we wouldn't get the view. Getting dressed, heading to work...they're your banker, your barista, your bowling instructor, they're everywhere, the surfers, the bros...hanging loose all over California, like low-hanging fruit.

GAR. Really?

PRITI. Oh, yeah, easy pickings. It's nice, it's like they provide a public service.

LEELA. They walk among us.

PRITI. The bros? Oh hell yes. Welcome to Orange County. They're all here. They're all everywhere.

LEELA. They're the humans. The gods are in the humans. The demons too. They're all here.

PRITI. Yeah. Part of the package, I guess. Being humans.

GAR. (*To* **PRITI**.) I'm okay with the package.

> (**PRITI** *and* **GAR** *have a moment.*)

LEELA. I'm okay with the package too.

PRITI. (*To* **LEELA**.) Oh, hey, I almost forgot, I got you this –

> (**PRITI** *pulls out an orange.*)

Gar said you wanted one, but he didn't have his wallet, so...

LEELA. You bought an orange?

PRITI. No, I stole it from that tree outside the India Mart. With the crazy dude?

Buy local, right? Or steal. Whatever.

LEELA. Oh. It's not sprayed.

PRITI. So what?

LEELA. So you shouldn't eat it.

PRITI. Who says? You gonna listen to them rules?

Look, there's no bugs or nothing. I mean that's why they spray, to keep the bugs off, right? Look at it, it's perfect. It's a fruit, you're supposed to eat it, from a tree, which has got to be better than from a supermarket. I mean what the hell? They can't actually forbid us from eating fruit on public property.

Besides, what's gonna happen if you take a bite? It's not like it's the tree of knowledge and if we eat it we get banished from Eden or something. Actually so what if it is, we eat it and it's the end of paradise on earth? I'm cool with that, this place is not that perfect.

GAR. That'd be crazy if we ended paradise.

PRITI. Yeah, my mom would be so pissed.

        (*Beat.* **LEELA** *contemplates the orange.*)

GAR. I could drive out to visit you, like maybe in a few months?

PRITI. Yeah...?

GAR. I mean once she eats that orange we'll all be banished anyway. You can't un-eat an orange. You're just out there in the cold harsh world with no one at your back, and the straight-up unknown ahead.

With just some, you know, citrus in your system, which is good for stuff.

PRITI. Like scurvy.

GAR. Yep.

LEELA. And skin, and blood vessels, and ligaments.

PRITI. Right. So we should be fine.

GAR. You ready for this, Leel?

LEELA. Yes.

PRITI. We're eating the orange?

LEELA. We're eating the orange.

GAR. We're eating the orange!

>   (**LEELA** *peels the orange.*)

LEELA. What beach is this?

PRITI. No clue.

GAR. This is really good. This is a good morning on a good beach.

>   (*They eat.*)

PRITI. Oh my god, this orange is amazing.

GAR. Better be, since it's the apocalypse. The apocalypse orange. Who knew it'd be us?

PRITI. My mom.

GAR. So true.

PRITI. God, I'm in so much shit. We need to find a phone to tow my sister's car.

>   (*They all eat the orange and watch the sunrise. Scene transforms to...*)

Scene Thirteen: The Wedding

(The wedding. FATHER *faces* LEELA *and* PRITI.*)*

[Illustration: Orange marigold wedding garlands bedeck the room.]

FATHER. *(To* LEELA.*)* Look at me when I am talking to you!

PRITI. Okay so listen, it's all my fault, I dragged her out and then we lost track of time

FATHER. You need to shut up. Your own parents will deal with you. You can leave now.

PRITI. No, I don't want to leave, none of this is Leela's fault.

FATHER. You are not to communicate with Leela again!

PRITI. Wait, what?

FATHER. Leela! Leela, pay attention, this girl is not your friend, she took you along as a joke with her real friends! You understand?

PRITI. That's actually not true.

FATHER. I have asked you to leave.

PRITI. And you can't just tell me not to talk to her, that's nuts.

FATHER. Leave!

> *(Beat.* PRITI *pulls out the brown paper bag, it contains glass bangles.)*

PRITI. Yo Leel, these are for you and your mom. From my sister...well from our whole family. Thank you for coming to the wedding. I'm really glad you came.

FATHER. I'll take those.

PRITI. They're for her!

> *(*LEELA *accepts the bangles.)*

LEELA. Thank you, we appreciate your generosity.

PRITI. Yeah. I mean they're glass.

LEELA. I like them.

PRITI. Yeah. Shit. I didn't... I mean I should have gotten the good ones, I was just...

FATHER. Alright, let's go.

LEELA. *(To* **PRITI.***)* You're crying again.

PRITI. Yeah, I don't know why, jesus.

LEELA. It means you love me.

PRITI. That's...

 Yeah...

 Right. Cousins.

LEELA. Cousins.

PRITI. Um. So don't let anyone disappear you or anything, 'cause I'll just come kidnap you again.

LEELA. Okay.

PRITI. Okay.

 (To **FATHER.***)* She was totally my hostage. Leela didn't do anything wrong.

  (PRITI *exits.)*

FATHER. I asked you to be discrete, that is all I asked of you. Do you understand me?

LEELA. Yes.

FATHER. You did not do what I asked.

  (MOTHER *enters, unnoticed by* **FATHER.***)*

LEELA. I went on an adventure. An adventure is not hotel rooms and airplanes. An adventure is when you go exploring on your own and things happen.

FATHER. You are not like other children. You can't have adventures, you cannot be alone, not since you were small. Your mother and I...

LEELA. I can. I can be alone. I was alone. And the gods did not come, no one came to help me, and it was okay. I can be alone.

FATHER. You understand that those stories your grandfather told you were made-up, right? The gods and the demons, those are just stories.

MOTHER. She knows that.

FATHER. What?

MOTHER. She knows that they're made-up, they're parables.

LEELA. Stories are how humans understand the world.

MOTHER. That's right.

LEELA. And parables are better than metaphors. I'm hungry.

FATHER. You see how she cannot be here? Huh? This is your problem now!

MOTHER. *(To* FATHER.*)* What are you doing here, Deep? What are you doing living here in California instead of with us? I'll tell you what, you are just like your daughter, your head is in the clouds, but you're doing it on purpose. Pretending that your life is something it is not...

FATHER. I'm not –

MOTHER. ...Why are we at this hotel? Why are we not staying at your flat? In our home.

FATHER. How is this relevant to this conversation?

MOTHER. This is very relevant to this conversation!

FATHER. This is not important! It's stupid! I moved. I moved to a smaller flat, alright? I don't need the large one for just myself.

(MOTHER *takes this in. Then...)*

MOTHER. You could live with us, in Calcutta, here, wherever. But you don't, you don't want to be with us. You prefer to live in your fantasy, your unhappy fantasy. Is it so much better than your unhappy reality? Because I don't have your ability for denial, I am here in the unhappy reality, and Leela and I...and I am feeling very alone.

(Beat.)

LEELA. Ask her why.

(FATHER *looks at* LEELA.*)*

You should ask her why she feels alone. That's a social cue, you should ask her.

(FATHER *does not.)*

MOTHER. Are you with us, Deep? Are you with us or not? Choose. Choose now.

(A suspended moment between them. Sound of airplane hum rises...)

LEELA. Three humans standing in a room. One walks out...

*(**FATHER** exits. The room and the family.)*

And then there's...

(Airplane hum gets louder. Scene transforms to...)

Scene Fourteen: In Air

[Illustration: The airplane window from Scene One, now with shading and color.]

*(**MOTHER** and **LEELA** on the plane, like at beginning. The only difference is that **LEELA** now wears the bangles she received from Priti. Loud airplane hum. They sit for a few beats, **LEELA** stares out window. Then...)*

*(Airplane hum drops. **LEELA** hands **MOTHER** her notebook.)*

MOTHER. What's this?

LEELA. My drawings of Orange County.

MOTHER. Okay, thank you darling.

> *(**MOTHER** flips through.)*

[Illustrations: Square, circle, two diamonds, narrow rectangle, circle, oval.]

(The "oval" lingers for the rest of the play.)

Okay, I'll look at it more later.

> *(**LEELA** nods. Silence. **LEELA** looks out the window.)*

LEELA. The black box is orange so you can find it.

MOTHER. Hmm.

LEELA. But even if you find it and listen to the whole recording, you'll never understand everything.

MOTHER. No that's true. You want some juice?

LEELA. You can listen to it over and over, but it's still just a black box that is orange. It's not the person who is missing.

> *(Long pause.)*

MOTHER. I'm not... Leela, I'm not missing anyone. I'm not missing any person. I have you. You are here, and I'm not trying to find anyone else. No one is missing.

LEELA. Okay.

MOTHER. No one is missing, Leela. You are all that I want for a daughter. I want nothing more.

LEELA. I don't think I'll be like other people even if I practice.

MOTHER. I know that.

LEELA. Okay.

MOTHER. Okay.

Nothing is missing. No one is missing. I know I'm always looking for...for the black box that is orange... I can't promise to stop looking, but...you must know that nothing is missing. You are perfect.

I just get lonely sometimes when you're elsewhere. In the clouds. But that is my own problem. Okay? Okay?

> (*A very, very, very long silence. With airplane noise.*)

LEELA. Okay.

> (*Airplane noise rises. Loud. Blackout.*)

End of Play

[Handwritten note:] For a moment, my head was in the clouds. In this temporal world. I was Leela, Pritti, and bar. I was brought into a world where I could feel the clouds, the wind, the raving oceans, the kisses of a loved one. How wonderful it is to find these specks of life. Why is it that the animals simply don't feel the same to me?